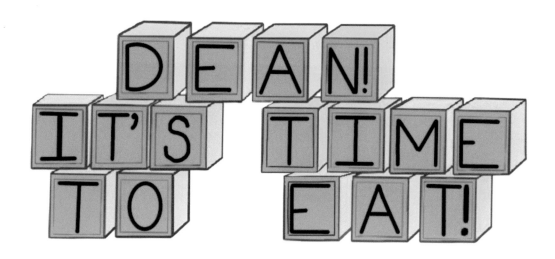

MONICA EUSTACHE

For the Trilogy.

ISBN: 9798392123964

On a very nice day, and not one in particular, brothers, Sean and Vaughn, decided to make dinner. Once it was finished, they called to their little brother...

DEAN!"

CALLED, SEAN.

"IT'S TIME TO EAT!".

"IT'S TIME TO EAT!". VAUGHN, SANG EXCITEDLY.

7

First, Sean and Vaughn looked inside their toy chest...

... and they didn't see Dean.

They went outside. ∫

He wasn't on the left.

And ~ he wasn't on the ~ right.

NOT DEAN

They checked right here.

They even checked way over there!

THEY FLOATED ALL THE WAY UP...

... and swam all the way down.
But, Dean was nowhere to be found.

Can you believe they even went flying into the future and still didn't see Dean?

And when the past
was a blast, Dean was
pooped out! So, he took
a nap on a new friend's back,
while his brothers rode free
through the weeds and a breeze.

20

They even searched where it was . . .

"Let's get out of here!" the boys screamed.
So, the boys ran and ran straight into a…

Freezing Snowstorm

"Vaughn! How come these snowflakes look like snowballs?" laughed, Sean.

"I'm uncertain, Sean! But, I wish that Dean was here- he LOVES to throw snowballs!" laughed, Vaughn.

While the boys thawed out in the shining hot sun,
Dean tried to get the attention of his brothers.
But, yet again, Sean and Vaughn didn't see him.

After a bit of excitement, the boys were wiped out!
So, they took a quiet little stroll, down a quiet little block.
And standing out there with a brown fence at it's feet,
was a big ole goat, known by the name of Boat.
" Excuse us, Mr. Boat," said, Sean.
"Have you seen our brother, D-"

screamed, Boat. "Who is *that*?"
The boys laughed so hard that
Sean fell to the ground!

In what felt like a search that lasted ten years,
just 15 minutes passed and Dean was nowhere near!
So, they headed home in hopes he'd be there.

"I'M RIGHT BEHIND YOU!" LAUGHED, DEAN.

Sean, Vaughn and Dean finally
made it home to eat.

And they ate every bite.

Fin.

Things to find:

BOAT

STOP

Titan

Never give up.